MW01622353

Roberto Bolaño

A Little Lumpen Novelita

TRANSLATED BY NATASHA WIMMER

Roberto Bolaño (1953–2003) was the author of *The Savage Detectives* and *2666*, among many other notable works. Born in Santiago, Chile, he later lived in Mexico City, Paris, and Barcelona. His accolades include the National Book Critics Circle Award and the Premio Rómulo Gallegos. He died at the age of fifty and is widely considered to be the greatest Latin American writer of his generation.

Natasha Wimmer is a translator of contemporary fiction and literary nonfiction. She is a regular visiting lecturer at Princeton University and Columbia University, and she has written reviews and criticism for *The New York Times* and *The New York Review of Books*, among other publications.

Roberto Bolaño

A Little Lumpen Novelita

Also by Roberto Bolaño

Collected Poetry
Cowboy Graves
The Spirit of Science Fiction
Woes of the True Policeman
Posthumous Stories
The Third Reich
The Insufferable Gaucho
The Return
Antwerp
Monsieur Pain
The Skating Rink
2666
Nazi Literature in the Americas
The Savage Detectives
Amulet
Last Evenings on Earth
Distant Star
By Night in Chile

A Little Lumpen Novelita

Roberto Bolaño

A Little Lumpen Novelita

Translated from the Spanish by
NATASHA WIMMER

Picador
Farrar, Straus and Giroux • New York

Picador
120 Broadway, New York 10271

EU Representative: Macmillan Publishers Ireland Ltd, 1st Floor, The Liffey Trust Centre, 117–126 Sheriff Street Upper, Dublin 1, DO1 YC43

Printed in the United States of America
Originally published in 2002 by Mondadori, Spain, as *Una novelita lumpen*
English translation originally published in 2014 by New Directions, by arrangement with the Heirs of Roberto Bolaño and the Andrew Wylie Agency, New York
First Picador paperback edition, 2025

Library of Congress Cataloging-in-Publication Data
Names: Bolaño, Roberto, 1953–2003 author | Wimmer, Natasha translator
Title: A little lumpen novelita / Roberto Bolaño ; translated from the Spanish by Natasha Wimmer.
Other titles: Novelita lumpen. English
Description: First Picador paperback edition. | New York : Picador, 2025.
Identifiers: LCCN 2025030105 | ISBN 9781250338570 paperback
Subjects: LCSH: Young women—Fiction | Orphans—Fiction | Life change events—Fiction | Criminals—Fiction | Rome (Italy)—Fiction | LCGFT: Fiction | Novels
Classification: LCC PQ8098.12.O38 N6813 2025
LC record available at https://lccn.loc.gov/2025030105

10 9 8 7 6 5 4 3 2 1

for Lautaro and Alexandra Bolaño

All writing is garbage.

People who come out of nowhere to try and put into words any part of what goes on in their minds are pigs.

All writers are pigs. Especially writers today.

Antonin Artaud

Now I'm a mother and a married woman, but not long ago I led a life of crime. My brother and I had been orphaned. Somehow that justified everything. We didn't have anyone. And it all happened overnight.

Our parents died in a car accident on the first vacation they took without us, on a highway near Naples, I think, or some other horrible southern highway. Our car was a yellow Fiat, a used car, but it looked like new. After the accident it was just a tangle of gray steel. When I saw it at the police yard with the other wrecked cars, I asked my brother about the color.

"Wasn't it yellow?"

My brother said yes, of course it had been yellow, but that was before. Before the accident. Collisions warp color or warp the way we see color. I didn't know what he meant by that. I asked him. He said: Light . . . color . . . everything. Poor guy, I thought, he's taking it harder than me.

That night we slept at a hotel and the next day we took the train back to Rome, with what was left of our parents. We were escorted by a social worker, or a counselor, or a psychologist, I don't know, my brother asked her what she was and I didn't hear the answer because I was looking out the window.

The only people at the burial were an aunt, my mother's sister, along with her horrible daughters. I stared at my aunt the entire time (which wasn't long) and more than once I thought I caught a half-smile on her lips, or sometimes a whole smile, and then I knew (though actually I'd known all along) that my brother and I were alone in the world. The ceremony was brief. Outside the cemetery we kissed our aunt and cousins and that was the last we saw of them. As we were walking to the nearest metro station I said to my brother that my aunt had smiled—meaning that she might as well have come right out and laughed—as the coffins were slid into their niches. He said that he had noticed it too.

After that, the days were different. Or the passing of the days. Or the thing that joins one day and the next but at the same time marks the boundary between them. Suddenly the night stopped existing and everything was constant sun and light. At first I thought it was exhaustion, or the shock of our parents' sudden disappearance, but when I told my brother about it he said that he had noticed the same thing. Sun and light and an explosion of windows.

I began to think that we were going to die.

But our life followed the same patterns as it had before our parents' death. Each morning we went to school. We talked to the people we thought of as friends. We did our schoolwork. Not much, but some. After we filled out a few simple forms, our father's pension was transferred to us. We thought we were going to get more and we filed a complaint. One morning, in front of a bureaucrat who was trying to explain that my father had earned X amount of money while he was alive and why we were due less than half of that after his death, my brother started to cry. He swore at the clerk and I had to drag him out of the office. It isn't fair, he yelled. It's the law, I heard the clerk say, sounding sorry for us.

I looked for work. Each morning I bought the newspaper and read the Help Wanted columns in the schoolyard, underlining whatever looked interesting. In the afternoon, after eating any old thing, I left the house and didn't come back until I had stopped at each place. The listings, whether they spelled it out or not, were mostly for escorts, but I'm no prostitute. I used to lead a life of crime, but I was never a prostitute.

One day I found a job at a salon. I washed hair. I didn't do any cutting, but I watched how the other girls did it and I prepared for the future. My brother said that it was stupid to work, that we could live happily on the pension we got from the government, on the income of our orphanhood. Orphanhood, ridiculous word. We started to add things up. We really could get by, but only by going without almost everything. My brother said that he could give up eating three meals a day. I looked at him and I couldn't tell whether he was serious or not.

"How many times a day do you eat?"

"Three. Four."

"And how many times a day are you saying you're willing to eat from now on?"

"Once."

A week later my brother found a job at a gym. At night, when he got home, we talked and made plans. I dreamed about having my own hair salon. I had reason to think that the future was in small salons, small boutiques, small record stores, tiny exclusive bars. My brother said the future was in computers, but since he worked at a gym (sweeping floors and cleaning bathrooms), he'd started lifting weights and doing all the things people do to build their bodies.

Gradually we gave up on getting an education. Sometimes I didn't go to school in the mornings (the incessant light was unbearable). Other times it was my brother who didn't go. As the days went by we both ended up staying home in the mornings, yearning for school but incapable of going out, getting on the bus, walking into our respective classrooms, and opening the books and notebooks from which we would learn nothing.

We killed time watching TV, first the talk shows, then cartoons, and finally the morning shows with interviews and news about famous people. But more about that later. TV and videos play an important role in this story. Even today, when I turn on the TV, I seem to get a glimpse of my criminal younger self, but the vision doesn't last long, no longer than the time it takes the TV to fully come on. For an instant, though, I can see the eyes of the person I used to be, my hair, my scornful lips, my cold-looking cheekbones, and my neck, cold too, like marble. The sight always gives me a shiver.

Around this time, because of his job at the gym, my brother developed a strange habit.

"Want to see how I'm doing?" he would ask.

Then he would take off his shirt and show me his muscles. Even though it was cold and the apartment wasn't heated, he'd take off his shirt or his T-shirt and show me the muscles that were timidly emerging from his body like tumors, protuberances that had nothing to do with him or with my image of him—of his scrawny adolescent body.

Once he told me that he dreamed of being Mr. Rome and then Mr. Italy or Master of the Universe. I laughed in his face and gave him my frank opinion. To be Master of the Universe you have to train from the time you're ten, I told him. I thought that bodybuilding was like chess. My brother said that if I could dream of owning a mini-salon, he had the right to dream of a better future too. That was the word he used: *future.* I went into the kitchen and got our dinner started. Spaghetti. Then I set out the plates and silverware. Still thinking. At last I said that I didn't care about the future, that I had ideas, but those ideas, if I really thought about it, never extended into the future.

"Where do they go, then?" howled my brother.

"Nowhere."

Then we would watch TV until we fell asleep.

Around four in the morning I usually woke with a start. I would get up from my chair, clear the dirty dishes from the table, wash them, straighten the living room, clean the kitchen, put another blanket over my brother, turn down the TV, go to the window and look out into the street with its double row of parked cars: I couldn't believe that it was still night, that this incandescence was night. It made no difference whether I closed my eyes or kept them open.

II

One day my brother rented an X-rated movie and we watched it together. It was horrible and I said so. He agreed. We watched the whole thing and then we watched TV, first an American series and then a game show. The next day my brother returned the movie and rented another one. It was X-rated too. I said that we didn't have enough money to rent movies every day. He didn't answer. When I asked him why he'd rented the same kind of movie again, he said it was to learn.

"Learn what?"

"Learn how to make love," said my brother without looking at me.

"Watching dirty movies isn't going to teach you anything," I said.

"Don't be so sure," he answered in a hoarse voice that I had never heard before.

His eyes were bright. Then he started to do exercises on the floor, sit-ups and other things, and for a second I thought he was going crazy. I shouldn't be so hard on him, I thought. I said that maybe he was right and I was wrong—maybe he was on the right track. "Are you still a virgin?" he asked me from the floor. "I am," I said. "Me too," he said. I said that was normal at his age.

The next night there was a new X-rated movie in the house. As we were watching it I fell asleep. Before I closed my eyes, I thought: I'm going to dream about this filth, but instead I dreamed about the desert. I was walking in the desert, dying of thirst, and on my shoulder there was a white parrot, a parrot that kept saying: "I can't fly, I'm sorry, please forgive me, but I can't fly." He was saying this because at some point in the dream I had asked him to fly. He weighed too much (ten pounds at least, he was a big parrot) to be carried for so long, but the parrot wouldn't budge, and I could hardly walk, I was shaking, my knees hurt, my legs, my thighs, my stomach, my neck, it was like having cancer, but also like coming—coming endlessly and exhaustingly—or like swallowing my eyes, my own eyes, swallowing them and at the same time trying not to bite down on them, and every so often the white parrot tried to help, saying: "Courage, Bianca," but mostly it kept its beak shut, and I knew that when I dropped on the hot sand and I was dying of thirst it would fly, fly away from this part of the desert to another part of the desert, fly away from my expiring flesh in search of other, less expiring flesh, fly away from my dead body forever, forever.

When I woke up my brother was asleep in his chair and the screen was a gray sea, gray and black stripes, as if a storm was approaching Rome and only I could see it.

Soon I was going along with my brother on his video store forays. In the mornings, during school hours, while kids our age were in class or shoplifting or getting high or having sex for money, I started to visit the video stores in our neighborhood and the surrounding neighborhoods, at first with my brother, who was trying to find the lost films of Tonya Waters, a porn star he had fallen in love with and whose adventures he was getting to know by heart, and then alone, though I didn't rent X-rated movies except when my brother had a special request, say for something featuring Sean Rob Wayne, who had worked twice with Tonya Waters and whose film career had thereby acquired a particular significance for my brother, as if anything that came into contact with Waters became automatically worthy of his attention.

Without surprise I discovered that I liked video stores. Not so much the ones in our neighborhood, but the stores in other neighborhoods. In that sense I was different from my brother, who only went to the video stores that were near home or on the way between our house and the gym where he worked. Familiarity was a source of comfort for my poor brother.

I, on the other hand, liked to try new places, plasticky sanitized stores with lots of customers, or dubious establishments with a single Balkan or Asian clerk, where no one knew anything about me. In those days I felt something that wasn't quite happiness but that did resemble enthusiasm, wandering streets I had hardly ever been down and that invariably ran into Via Tiburtina or Trajan's Park. Sometimes I went into a video store and spent half an hour or more scanning the shelves of video cases and then I would leave without renting anything, not because I wouldn't have liked to, but because I had no money.

Other times, throwing caution to the wind, I'd rent two movies at once. I was omnivorous: I liked romance (which almost always made me laugh), classic horror, gore, psychological horror, crime horror, military horror. Sometimes I sat for a long time on Garibaldi Bridge or on a bench on Tiber Island, next to the old hospital, and I studied the video cases as if they were books.

Some cars would slow down as they passed. I heard whispers, which I ignored. Usually people would roll down the window and say something, make some promise, and then keep going. There were cars that passed and didn't stop. There were cars that passed with the windows already rolled down and kids inside yelling—"Fascism or barbarism!"—and they'd keep going too. I didn't look at them. I stared at the river and my videos and tried to forget the few things I knew.

III

One evening my brother came home with two men. They weren't his friends, though my brother chose to think they were. One was from Bologna, the other from Libya or Morocco. But they looked like twins. Same head, same nose, same eyes. They reminded me of a clay bust I had seen recently in a magazine at the salon. They spent the night.

"But where will they sleep?" I said to my brother. "There's no room."

He gave me a haughty look, as if to say he had the situation under control.

"In our parents' bedroom," he said.

He was right, there was room. The men slept there.

I went to bed early. I didn't feel like watching my favorite shows.

I hardly slept a wink. When I got up at six in the morning, the kitchen was clean. The men had washed the pots, the dishes, and the silverware and left it all on the rack to dry. The ashtrays were empty and clean. I think they even swept before they went to bed. I thought about that as I ate breakfast and then I went to work, though it was very early and I spent almost two hours wandering around the neighborhood.

When I got back they were still there. They had made a spinach purée and a spicy tomato sauce. The table was set. In the refrigerator were two big bottles of beer. It was only then, as we ate, that I learned their names. They introduced themselves. But I don't remember the names anymore and I'd rather not make an effort to remember them. My brother looked nervous and happy. The two men looked relaxed. The Bolognan even pulled out a chair for me.

That night I realized how alike they were, and that night, too, they told me that they weren't brothers, though many people thought they were. The Libyan said something that at the time I found mysterious. In a way, he said, those people weren't wrong. Silly as it may seem, people are never wrong. Even if we look down on them, and sometimes rightly so, people are *never* wrong. That's our curse, he said.

"Are you brothers or not?" I asked.

The Libyan said that they were blood brothers.

"Did you swear a blood oath, did you cut your palms and rub the blood together? Is that what you mean?"

That's what they meant. My brother thought it was great that there were still people who swore blood oaths. I thought it was childish. The Libyan said he agreed with me, but I think he only agreed to be polite, since if he thought it was childish, why had he done it? Unless they'd known each other since they were children, which they hadn't.

That night I watched TV with them for a while.

My brother had met them at the gym, where they did some kind of work that was never clear to me. Sometimes I got the impression that they were trainers, a job with a certain prestige, and other times that they were just sweepers and errand boys, like my brother. Either way, they were always talking about the gym, like people who come home and can't stop going on about work. They talked about the gym—and so did my brother, with a fervor new to me—and about protein diets and meals with names that had the ring of science fiction, like Fuel Tank 3000 or Weider energy bars (all the nutrients you need for the body of a champion!).

This went on until I told them that if they wanted to keep talking they should do it in the kitchen because I couldn't hear my game show. I liked (I still like) to listen carefully to the questions and answers because that way while I'm being entertained I learn something that probably won't help me in any way but that seems worth knowing. Sometimes I get an answer right. When that happens I start to think that maybe I could go on TV and be a contestant. But then more questions come and I don't know any of the answers, which is when I realize that I'm better off here, on this side of the screen, because if I were there, in front of the cameras, I'd probably just make an ass of myself.

The surprising thing, though, was that when I asked them to stop talking, they stopped. And then we were all quiet watching the show, which was at the most exciting part: there were only two contestants left, an older man, maybe forty or fifty, and a girl with little glasses and a face that was too serious, kind of scrunched up. She had incredible hair, shoulder-length and shiny, all silky black. For a minute I imagined her sitting in the salon. Ugly thoughts. I tried to wipe them from my mind.

Then the girl was asked to define the word *nimbus*. And the Bolognan, next to me, said that it was a halo, the circle of light around a saint's head. And before the girl could open her mouth, he added that it was also a low cloud formation, a cluster of cumulous clouds.

I stared at the Bolognan and I stared at the TV. My brother smiled, as if he knew the answer too, though I knew he didn't. And time ticked away and the girl lost her turn and it was the older man's turn and he said that a nimbus was, in fact, a low cloud. And when the host, to give the old guy a hard time, asked "And what else, sir?," the man was silent and couldn't think of anything else.

And then came more contestants and more questions and the Bolognan answered almost all of them, some of them wrong, admittedly, but most of them right, and my brother—and even I—said that he should try out for the show, he could make a shitload of money (though I didn't use that word), and then my brother told me that his friend was always doing crossword puzzles and he actually finished them, unlike the average person, who would start a puzzle and leave it half-done, and it seemed to me that it was one thing to be able to finish crossword puzzles and another thing to be a game-show winner, but I kept my mouth shut, because clearly the Bolognan could win any quiz show he signed up for.

But then I stopped to think: When had my brother seen his friend doing crossword puzzles? Because if anything was clear it was that they knew each other from the gym where my brother worked and the Bolognan worked and even the Libyan worked, mopping floors, scrubbing lockers and showers, sweeping the weight room or selling energy drinks, all tasks incompatible with a leisurely activity like solving crossword puzzles, which—as everybody knows—is something that's done when you have nothing else to do.

That night, when I was in bed and the house was quiet, I imagined—or rather saw—my brother and his two friends at Rome's Central Station sitting in the cafeteria waiting, my brother and the Libyan doing nothing, watching people come in and out, and the Bolognan working the crossword puzzle from the *L'Osservatore Romano*, a right-wing paper no matter how you look at it, though he claimed it was an anarchist paper, a superfluous and therefore futile explanation or excuse. Once I saw him with *Tutto Calcio* under his arm and I said "That's what you read," a simple statement of fact, not meaning anything else by it, and he said yes, I read *Tutto Calcio*, but it isn't a right-wing paper the way people think it is, it's an anarchist paper.

As if I cared what newspapers he read or didn't read.

My father read *Il Messagiero*. My brother and I didn't read anything (it was a luxury we couldn't afford). I don't know which papers are right-wing and which are left-wing. But the Bolognan was always justifying himself. It was part of who he was, and also part of his charm, or so he thought. But as I was saying, I was in bed with the lights out and the covers pulled up to my chin, in the silence of the night, a silence that looked yellow to me, and I saw my brother and his two friends in a bar at Central Station, sitting around a table with three glasses of beer and looking bored, because waiting is terrible and they were waiting for something that wasn't coming, but was about to come, or at least that was what they were betting on, the three of them, and while they were sitting there the Bolognan had more than enough time to finish a crossword puzzle, from *L'Osservatore Romano* or *La Repubblica* or *Il Messagiero*. And imagining this scene, I was overcome by an infinite sadness.

I felt a weight on my chest, a pain in my heart, a sense of anguish. As if a fog were rising from the underground tunnels and swamping the whole of Central Station, and I was the only one who could see it (but I wasn't there). As if the fog was blurring my brother's face and coming irrevocably between us. But then I fell asleep and I forgot or dismissed what I had seen—or what I had foreseen, because it really was a premonition.

And so the days went by.

IV

One morning the Bolognan and the Libyan left. I spent an hour, more or less, going through the drawers to see whether they'd stolen anything. Nothing was missing.

Even I couldn't deny that their conduct had been impeccable for the five days they'd stayed with us. They always washed the dishes, three times they made dinner themselves, and they didn't try anything with me, which was important. I could sense the interest in their eyes, in the way they moved, and the way they talked to me, but I also noted their self-control and found it flattering.

I'd only had one boyfriend in my life and we had broken up shortly before my parents' car accident on that terrible southern highway.

My boyfriend lived nearby and was the same age as me, so it wasn't long before I saw him with another girl, both of them looking happy, near the entrance to a club. I was on my way home from my job at the salon, it was a Saturday, and I was walking in a daze, staring up at the sky, which—as I've said—looked stranger every day. My ex-boyfriend was with his new girlfriend, propped on the wall outside the club, and when he saw me go by he said my name. I lowered my eyes and there he was. He was smiling a friendly smile. I smiled at him too. He asked if I had dropped out of school. I didn't answer. I thought for a second that the logical thing would be to stop and talk to him and his new girlfriend, but instead I kept walking. When I had gone a little way I stared up at the sky again and I had the feeling that I was living on another planet.

So much for that.

You couldn't say I'd gained much experience with my boyfriend. He was an ordinary guy and I liked him and then one day I stopped liking him. That was all. With the Bolognan (and the Libyan) it was different, because they shared meals with us, slept in my parents' room, and watched me from up close in a way that no one (except my brother) ever had. What do they *see*? I wondered. What face, what eyes do they see? I didn't wonder this very often, but once or twice I did. Now I know that there's no such thing as closeness. One person's eyes are always shut. The first person sees and the second doesn't. Or the second person sees and the first doesn't. Only a mother can be close, but that was unknown territory back then. A blank space. There was only the illusion of closeness.

And the closeness of my brother's friends, a closeness built on the basis of glances and small gestures, among other things, wasn't just flattering; I liked it, too. Let me explain: I was no one's slave; I was the arbiter of them all. I was blind, but I was the yardstick by which they measured their freedom. It sounds stupid, but that's how it felt and I'm sure they intended it that way. They didn't swear in front of me, they weren't like my brother, they took out the garbage, they always raised the toilet seat, unlike even my late father, a silent and considerate man.

But I don't want to talk about my father. I want to talk about my brother's friends and about the evening or night when I went through the drawers to see whether they had taken anything when they left. My brother saw me, I remember, and said with uncharacteristic certainty: "They didn't take anything. They're legal. They're my friends." But I still inspected the whole house, room by room, even searching the bathroom to see whether anything was gone, a bottle of cologne. Nothing. My brother was right.

Then a week went by and then another and my brother hardly mentioned his friends.

One night, as we were watching TV, he said that they were in Milan at a bodybuilding competition. Mr. Italy. I laughed.

"In Frosinone, maybe," I said.

My brother looked at me, confused. What was I trying to say? That they might be able to make it in Frosinone, but not Milan? Maybe. I could imagine them anywhere else in Italy—Cosenza or Catanzaro, say—but not in Milan.

After that my brother stopped telling me things about them. I was someone—I realize now—who liked to face things head-on, whereas my brother and his friends wandered real and imaginary places with their heads down. But facing things head-on meant being consumed. I was being consumed.

I worked, did the shopping, cooked, watched TV, went with my brother to rent videos. Some nights I looked out the window and the night was as bright as day. Sometimes I thought that I was losing my mind, that it couldn't be normal, such brightness, but deep down I knew I would never lose my mind.

I was waiting for something. A catastrophe. A visit from the police or the social worker. The approach of a meteorite, darkening the sky. My brother rented Tonya Waters movies and I washed heads and nothing happened.

One day they came back.

My brother didn't mention it, maybe he didn't know they were coming back either. They were there one night when I got home from work. The three of them were sitting on the couch watching TV. I looked them straight in the face and asked how things had gone in Milan. The Libyan got up and shook my hand. The Bolognan nodded irritably and didn't get up from the couch. I could tell by their expressions that things hadn't gone well. So I didn't ask again. We ate together. We watched TV together. That night, while I was in bed thinking about them (or to be precise, thinking about their battered faces, shiny as if they'd been washed by force, as if a dark hand had dashed a bucket of water at them and then scoured them mercilessly, faces as wet and tired as if they'd returned from Frosinone on foot or in chains), while I was in bed, as I was saying, with the lights out and my eyes open, sure I would never fall asleep, one of them came into the room and made love to me. I think it was the Bolognan.

Then I asked again:

"How was Milan?"

And he said, "Bad, it was bad," as he put something on his penis and penetrated me. I think it was a condom but I can't say for sure.

The next morning, before I went to work, I looked for the used condom and couldn't find it. So maybe it was a condom that he put on and maybe it was something else. But what? I'll never know and now I don't care, but back then, that morning, as I was getting dressed and making the bed, I thought about that and about danger and love and all the seemingly strange things that turn up when you least expect them and that are actually pretexts for something different, something else (attainable things, not unattainable things), and then I went to work, the others were sleeping, my brother in his room, his two friends in my parents' old room, and the streets I walked didn't look like yesterday's streets, though I knew they were the same, streets don't change overnight, maybe in some places they do, but I've never been to those places, maybe in Africa, but not here, here I was the one who was changing, but when I got to the salon I realized that I hadn't changed, that the streets had shifted slightly, to the left or to the right, up or down, but I was still the same.

In my defense I can say—if anything needs to be said, if the notion of defense is pertinent (which it isn't)—that at no moment did I think that I was falling in love. I saw the shadowy negative of romantic situations. I saw the negative of passionate moments whose point of reference was always a TV series or the whispering of girls now forgotten. Sometimes I saw the negative of a whole life: a bigger house, a different neighborhood, children, a better job, time passing, old age, a grandchild, death in the public hospital or covered with a sheet in my parents' bed, a bed that I would have liked to hear creak, like an ocean liner as it goes down, but that instead was silent as a tomb.

That night I made love again with one of my brother's friends and the next night and the night after that too, and every night that week and the week after, until it began to show on my face that I was making love every night or that I wasn't sleeping much, to the point that my friends at work asked what was wrong, whether I was sick or what.

Then I looked in the mirror and I saw that I had circles under my eyes, that my face was pale, as if the moon, which shone as brightly for me as the sun, was affecting me. And then I decided that I didn't need to make love every night and I locked my door.

Life, despite what I expected, continued unchanged.

V

What did I expect? Back then I must not have been completely sane, because I expected tears.

That was what I expected. But there wasn't a single tear. They knocked at my door, many times, night after night, but neither of them cried.

Sometimes, as I was washing hair or sweeping the hallway at the salon, I imagined them waiting for me at home, patient in a way that was not of this world or at least not of the world that I knew, doing nothing but watching TV while my brother and I worked and brought home food and paid the bills that had to be paid. I imagined them sitting silently on the couch or I saw them doing push-ups and all those exercises they did to keep in shape, on the rug or by the balcony that overlooked Piazza Sonnino, as the day slowly faded and the light of the moon grew more intense, until it flooded night's farthest corners with a blinding light.

They'll never leave, I thought then.

Other times I thought: they'll leave without telling us, one day we'll come home and they'll be gone.

But when I got home they were always there, the house spotless, because they made it their job to cheerfully do everything that I used to do. Cheerfully, I say, and gladly, though I knew perfectly well that it was a fake cheer, as fake as mine, that their apparent goodwill hid feelings of emptiness, of sadness and grief in the face of the void. But they worked around the house. Dinner was always ready, the bathroom scoured with bleach, the rooms tidy. As if with these gestures they were saying to me: we aren't shiftless, we seem shiftless but we aren't, in fact if it was up to us we would do everything we could to make you happy.

Once a week, sometimes twice, I let them into my room. I didn't need to say anything, I just had to be more talkative than usual or give them a meaningful look (or what at the time I imagined was a meaningful look) and they knew immediately that they could visit me that night and they would find the door open.

Other times I got home and found the table set for one—me—and a note from my brother saying that they would be home late, that they had urgent business to take care of on the other side of the city, that there was rice in the kitchen and chicken in the refrigerator. At the end there were always a few lines from the Bolognan (sometimes I thought the Libyan didn't know how to write, not that it matters), repeating what my brother had said and promising to take care of him.

After eating and washing the dishes, I would sit down to watch some game show on TV and I tried to imagine where they might be, what kind of mess they had gotten themselves into. Sometimes, sick of the desperation and greed parading by on the screen, I reread the note and compared my brother's handwriting to the Bolognan's. My brother's was fragile, clumsy, insecure. The Bolognan's handwriting was like a convict's handwriting. After studying it for a long time, I decided that it looked less like handwriting than like a tattoo. Sometimes I tried to remember the naked body of the Bolognan, I tried to remember whether he had tattooed anything on his own body—a letter, a word, or a picture—but I couldn't remember.

Deep down, I think I was afraid something bad would happen. I think I sensed that it was coming soon and I worried about my brother, whose fate seemed so bound up with his friends' fate. I didn't care what happened to them. They were older and they were used to hard times, but my brother was innocent and I didn't want anything to happen to him.

Every so often I had terrible dreams. I saw my parents walking along a southern highway, they didn't recognize me, I kept going, happy to be so changed, then I thought better of it and turned around, but now my parents had turned into worms dragging themselves away, one after the other, torturously along the pavement, below a sign that read REGGIO CALABRIA 33 KILOMETERS, and though I called them by name, begging them to answer, warning them that they wouldn't get far crawling like that, they didn't even turn their worm heads to give me a final glance and they continued impassively along their way. Once in a while a late-model car would drive by with the windows rolled down and the kids inside shouting "Fascism or barbarism!"

In the dream I was crying, but when I woke up my eyes were dry and if I jumped out of bed and looked at myself in the mirror, the grim expression on my face frightened even me.

Sometimes my brother's friends turned sullen. If I asked what was wrong, what the problem was, the answer was always the same: nothing's wrong, everything's fine, our luck is about to change. My brother listened and nodded. Sometimes their own words actually cheered them up, like a shot of some mood-boosting drug.

Then I would carry the dishes into the kitchen and ask whether they wanted coffee and they would say yes, we do, and I would make coffee and sit in the kitchen chewing mint gum, and I would contemplate the phrase "our luck is about to change," a phrase that meant nothing to me, no matter how much I turned it over in my head, because luck can't change, either it exists or it doesn't, and if it exists there's no way to change it, and if it doesn't exist we're like birds in a sandstorm, except that we don't realize it, of course, like in the Luciano Marchetti song: "The wind blows, we're birds in a storm, and nobody knows." Though I think there are people—very sad or unlucky people—who do know.

It's best not to think about these things. They're here, they touch us, they're gone, or they're here, they touch us, they swallow us up, and it's best—always—not to think about them. But I kept thinking, waiting for the coffee to be done, and I asked myself what my brother's friends meant by saying that their luck would change, how exactly they planned to change their luck (*their* luck, not mine or my brother's, though in a sense their luck would have an effect—any idiot could see that—on my brother's luck and maybe even mine), what they were ready to try, how far they were prepared to go to get their luck and ours to turn around.

At the same time economic conditions were deteriorating. Not much, but on TV they said they were deteriorating. Something was wrong in Europe or Italy, I think. Or Rome. Or our neighborhood. What I do know is that we barely had enough money to eat and one day my brother approached me with his friends trailing a few feet behind, as if not wanting to intrude on anything as intimate as a conversation between a brother and a sister, but also as if they couldn't resist the temptation to witness, even if at a prudent distance, my reaction to what my brother was going to say, which was already old news to them.

And what my brother said was that he wouldn't be working at the gym anymore. I asked whether he had quit. He said yes, in a way.

"Did you quit or were you fired?"

He admitted that he had been fired. When I asked him why he had been fired he said that he didn't know. Then he added that it wasn't surprising, that lots of young people lost their jobs overnight.

"But those people aren't orphans like us," I yelled, "those people have parents and can afford to be out of work for a while."

My brother said that when people started to get fired it didn't matter whether they were orphans or not. The Bolognan and the Libyan nodded in agreement. The understanding look on their faces turned my stomach. I stared through them as if they didn't exist. I asked my brother how we would manage on my salary alone. My brother shouted that it wasn't his fault. I told him not to yell, just because he was unemployed didn't mean he had to be rude, but my brother kept yelling and threatening people I had never heard of in my life and promising me that the situation was going to change, though he didn't explain how, and anyway I can't remember his promises because then I started to think about other things, and the Bolognan and the

Libyan took a step forward, or three steps, or maybe four steps, and they grabbed my brother, who had gone pale as a sheet, by the shoulders and the belt, I can't remember exactly, all I know is that the way they grabbed him gave me a bad feeling at the time, it's all right to grab someone by the shoulders, but grabbing him by the belt seemed excessive, my brother was upset but he wasn't out of control, he just kept yelling, probably so he wouldn't cry, but they grabbed him by the belt and dragged him into the living room or my parents' old room and I went into my room.

VI

To make a long story short: economic conditions deteriorated.

My salary wasn't enough to support four people and on top of that to cover the household expenses. One night I got home and the electricity had been turned off. It didn't matter to me, but we had to pawn my mother's wedding ring and several other things (that we never got back) to pay the bill and have electricity again so that we could at least watch TV.

One afternoon at the salon when there was nothing to do, I was flipping through a magazine and I found a quiz. It seemed to have been written just for me. The magazine was called *Donna Moderna* and it was the first time I had seen it. When I went home I took it with me and answered the questions.

"What do you think about men in their teens?"

They're like my brother, I guess. They don't have jobs. I like them.

"What do you think about men in their 20s?"

I don't know.

"What's a good age to die?"

Thirty-six, maybe. Before I turn forty.

"What actor would you date?"

Brad Pitt.

"What actor would you marry?"

Edward Norton.

"What actor would you choose as your lover?"

Antonio Banderas.

"What actor would you choose as your father?"

Robert De Niro.

"What actress would you choose as your best friend?"

Maria Grazia Cucinotta. (Surprising answer, because I always thought Maria Grazia Cucinotta looked superficial and egotistical, like someone who only cared about herself.)

"What actress would you be?"

Maria Grazia Cucinotta.

"Do you know anyone who would risk his life for you?"

No, I don't. And if I did, I'd do everything I could to change his mind. I'd tell him it wasn't worth risking his life for me. I'd reveal my true self and then he wouldn't want to have anything to do with me.

"If you were a bird, what kind of bird would you be?"

An owl.

"If you were a mammal, what kind of mammal would you be?"

A mole. Or a rat. In fact, I already live like a rat.

"If you were a fish, what kind of fish would you be?"

The kind that's used as bait. Once, when I was little, I saw a fisherman on Lake Albano, near Castel Gandolfo, where the Pope lives. He was fishing with a giant fishing rod and next to him he had a bucket and a little box. In the bucket were the fish he had just caught, three, I think, horrible, half dead, sandy black, and in the little box were the fish that the fisherman used as bait. They were tiny fish, translucent and silvery.

When I asked the fisherman if he had caught all of them, he answered that he hadn't, that some of them, the big ones, were the parents, and the little ones were the children. And that he had caught the big ones, and bought the little ones at a fishmonger's in Frascati. And that they weren't good to eat, they were only good as bait.

"What kind of geological feature would you be?"

A deep-sea trench.

"If you were a car, what kind of car would you be?"

A Fiat of flesh. (Not a good answer. What I'd really like to be is a vintage car, a Lamborghini. And I'd only leave the garage two or three times a year. I'd also like to be a Los Angeles taxi, the seats stained with semen and blood. Actually, I don't know how to drive and I couldn't care less about cars.)

"If you were a movie, what movie would you be?"

I'd be *War and Peace,* with Audrey Hepburn and Henry Fonda. I saw it a while ago on TV. And a strange thing happened: my brother and the Bolognan fell asleep. But the Libyan made it to the end and he said that he thought it was an amazing movie. I think so too, I said. Yes, I could tell, he said.

"If you had to kill someone, who would you kill?"

Whoever. I'd go over to the window and kill whoever.

"If you were a country, what country would you be?"

Algeria.

"Would you call yourself attractive?"

Yes.

"Would you call yourself intelligent?"

No.

"If you had to kill someone, what weapon would you choose?"

A gun. I had a friend at school who said she'd like to blow

up her boyfriend with an atomic bomb. I remember I thought that was really funny, because it wouldn't be just my friend's boyfriend who'd die, I would die too, and so would everyone in and around Rome, maybe even the fishermen of Frascati.

"How many children would you like to have?"

Zero.

VII

Saturdays and Sundays were the worst, because the four of us were home together and we had nothing to do. The rest of the week my brother and his friends went out to look for work (or so they said when I got home), but they never found anything, not even seasonal work, or the occasional odd job that might bring in a little money to help us get by.

At night, when I went to my room (they stayed up all hours watching TV), I thought about my parents, the accident, the winding southern highways, and everything seemed so far away that it made me weep with rage.

When that happened I jumped up, went back to the living room, motioned to one of my brother's friends (not caring whether my brother saw) and led him to my room, where we made love until I fell asleep and I could dream about other things, at least.

I didn't like my life. The nights were still crystal clear, but I had become less of an orphan and I was moving into an even more precarious realm where I would soon lead a life of crime.

What kind of crime? It didn't matter. It was all the same to me, though of course I knew that in the kingdom of crime there were many stages and levels and no matter how hard I tried, I would never reach the top.

I was afraid of becoming a prostitute. I didn't like the idea of it. But I sensed that it was all a matter of getting used to it. Sometimes while I was working at the salon, I clenched my fists and tried to imagine my future. Thief, assassin, drug dealer, black marketeer, con artist. No, probably not con artist, because con artists always have mentors and who would mine be? And I didn't like the idea of being a drug dealer either. I don't like drug addicts. I don't have anything against them, but dealing with drug addicts all day seemed unbearable (not anymore, now it doesn't seem so bad, now I think that in a way people who work with drug addicts are saints, and drug addicts are saints too). At moments of great exaltation I saw myself as a thief or an assassin. Deep down I knew it made most sense to be a prostitute.

Be that as it may, at the time I sensed that I was heading inexorably into the realm of crime and its nearness made me dizzy, intoxicated me, I slept badly, I had dreams in which nothing meant anything, unfettered dreams in which I had the courage to do what I wanted, though the things I did in dreams weren't exactly the things I would have done in real life, the things that appealed to me in real life.

Deep down I've always been an innocent. I'm an innocent now, and back then, when the nights were as bright as day, I was too. I didn't realize it, but I was. I looked at myself and I was blinded by the light from the mirror. My soul could find no repose. But I was an innocent, because if I hadn't been I would have been out of there like a shot and everything would be different now.

From here on my story gets even fuzzier.

VIII

For a few days I lived on tiptoe, I think. I went back and forth from work to home trying not to call attention to myself, and at night I watched some TV, not much, since I was gradually losing interest in the shows I used to see.

Sometimes the house was empty when I got home. Then I would eat in the kitchen, sitting on a white stool, staring at the white-tiled wall, counting the tiles from top to bottom, then counting the rows, then losing my place and starting over. I can say without irony that I was bored.

Sometimes I went into my parents' old bedroom. It still looked the same, and if by some miracle the ghosts (or zombies) of my parents had come through the door, they wouldn't have found a thing out of place.

But a few items provided evidence to the contrary.

There was a suitcase half-hidden behind a chair, and the frame of a backpack just visible on top of the wardrobe. The suitcase was well made, of leather, and inside it were clean clothes that might have belonged to either the Bolognan or the Libyan. In the backpack were dirty clothes, just a small bundle, because if there was one thing that could be said about my brother's friends, it was that they had an undeniable predilection for cleaning. I couldn't find a single personal item among their belongings. Not a letter or an address book or a photocopy of their Social Security papers. I guessed that they always carried their important documents around with them. Or they didn't have any. Or they didn't exist.

Around this time I remember a conversation with one of my friends at work. She was the same age as me, but she had a boyfriend, and one evening before we closed up the salon she started to talk about her future. For a second I thought I was losing my mind. I couldn't believe what I was hearing.

"Are you serious? Are you making this up?"

She was serious, but when she saw how upset I was she stopped talking and went over to the other end of the room, where she said something to a stylist who was taking a break, sitting in a chair, smoking a cigarette and watching the sunset. There was an expression of deep melancholy on the stylist's face. But the look on the other girl's face was malevolent, I thought. I was breathing hard, as if I'd run from one point to another in record time, and though the other girl laughed a few times, as if she couldn't believe her own words, she seemed afraid. The stylist listened without getting up from her chair. It was as if the girl's words were sliding off her face, a hard face without a hint of indulgence. That's what I remember. And I remember the sunset, a sunset of rose and ocher that crept all the way to the back of the salon, but never touched me.

That night I didn't cry on the way home, which was something I'd been doing for a while. It was as if when I left work I walked straight into a wind tunnel that made me cry for no reason. A tunnel that at first seemed to have only a physical effect, bringing on tears and nothing else, but rather than getting used to it, over the last few days I had been struck by a feeling of enormous sadness, a sadness that I could only handle by crying.

But that day, as if I glimpsed that my life was about to take a sharp turn, I didn't cry. I put on my sunglasses, left the salon, stepped into the tunnel, and didn't cry. Not a single tear.

My brother and the two men who lived in our house were waiting for me. I saw them from outside. The three of them were standing in the window, like fish in a fishbowl, watching the street. It took them a while to spot me there on the sidewalk, watching them.

I climbed slowly up the stairs. I closed the door and paused in the hallway. All of a sudden there they were, talking. I listened. What else could I do? Though I've forgotten what they said. They had a plan. That much I do remember. A hazy plan on which each of them, my brother included, had gambled his future, and to which each had added his bit, his personal touch, his vision of fate and the turns of fate.

I remember I listened to them and then I pushed past them into the living room and sat down, tired of taking in so much information at once. They followed me and were silent, expectant.

I said:

"Don't stop, it's a good idea, keep talking."

Maybe I didn't say it was a good idea. Maybe I said that I wanted to hear them out. (I thought we were all going to end up in jail, but I didn't tell them that—I'm not a killjoy.)

They smiled and obeyed. My brother seemed the most enthusiastic, as if it had been his idea, though I knew it hadn't. The Libyan seemed the most skeptical. But the three of them were committed to the plan and they clung to it like shipwrecked sailors, laying it all out for me and presenting it in the best possible light. It was something that would require only the tiniest sacrifice, a plan in which cleverness was key. It was the perfect coup, a scheme that would open the doors of a new life to us, that would get us a house on the beach, or a restaurant in Tangiers, or a gym up north.

When they were done talking I said that it sounded good to me. Then I got up and went to bed and fell asleep without eating dinner.

At five in the morning I woke up. I turned on the light, I leafed through old magazines, and for a while I mulled over what they had explained. So this is the life of crime, I thought without fear.

The next morning I didn't go to work, I got up early, went out, bought bread, and called in sick from a payphone. I don't know whether they believed me or not. I didn't care.

At midday, the Libyan and the Bolognan brought me to Maciste's house. That wasn't his name, but it was what everyone called him. To some he was Maciste, to others Mr. Maciste or Mr. Bruno, to others Mr. Universe. It depended. Most didn't call him anything because Maciste never left the house and no one knew him and many of those who had known him, personally or by name, had forgotten him.

The house was on Via Germanico. It was a two-story house, with a small, overgrown garden in front, flanked by two six- or seven-story buildings. There was a tall metal gate. The shutters were closed, as if no one lived there. The paint on the façade was peeling in places, which made the place look even more neglected, if possible. And yet as we walked up to the door, we didn't see mail on the ground or trash in the garden, which meant that someone did come occasionally to clean. Sometimes Maciste made an appearance at a gym on Via Palladio, according to the Bolognan, and sometimes someone was sent from the gym to fix a piece of Maciste's exercise equipment.

"In there," said the Bolognan as we were leaving, "he has a huge private gym set up just for him. Once I came with another guy to fix a weight rack and we got to be friendly. I came back twice, but I couldn't get past the door. Maciste doesn't trust anybody."

Then, as we talked that afternoon about what we would do, they told me that for a while, probably before my brother and I were born, Maciste had been a movie star and his movies were seen all over the world. Then he'd had the accident and retired, and after that he'd gradually been forgotten.

But Maciste wasn't the kind of person who's easy to forget. I, for one, know I'll never forget him. No matter what happens, I'll never forget him.

IX

His real name was Giovanni Dellacroce. This was something that neither the Bolognan nor the Libyan knew (let alone my brother, who because of his age and lack of skills plays a marginal role here, I'm afraid). His stage name was Franco Bruno. People called him Mr. Universe, because he had won the title twice in the early sixties, or Maciste, which was the name of the character he played in four or maybe five movies, all huge hits in Italy and around the world. He was born in Pescara, but had lived in Rome since he was fifteen, in Santa Loreto, a suburb that he thought of as home and for which he was sometimes nostalgic, though when luck was on his side, he bought the big house on Via Germanico where I met him the night I was brought there.

A night that was like high noon in August and was one of the strangest nights in my life.

The Bolognan rang the bell several times. A voice over an intercom asked who was there.

"Friends," said the Bolognan. No answer. The intercom might as well have been broken. After a while he rang again and said the name of the gym and the name—or so I thought I understood—of a mutual friend, and as if this weren't enough, he announced our full names, mine included.

Then the gate opened and we were let into the little garden where even at night the plants struggled for scarce living space. More than a garden, it was like a cemetery.

There were three stone steps up to the porch. For a long time we stood there waiting for someone to open the door.

The tension on the faces of my brother's friends, the tension and at the same time the joy, a primordial joy, pure and unwavering, is one of the things that comes back to me whenever I remember that night, and each time it does I try to brush it away, because it's a joy that I want neither for myself nor anywhere near me. It's a joy that comes too close to beggarliness, an explosion of beggarliness, and also to cruelty, indifference.

Then the door opened and we got a glimpse of a dark threshold where I seemed to see a shadow move very quickly, and a foyer, also dark, into which we stepped and out of which we backed like frightened children entrusted with a mysterious responsibility, and into which we stepped again, sheepishly, and out of which we inevitably backed again, until I took three steps inside, this time alone, and bumped into a piece of furniture and asked whether anyone was there.

A voice—Maciste's—told me to stay where I was, not to move forward or back, and then he greeted my brother's friends, hello, how are you? And in that brief *how are you* I sensed an incredible fragility, a fragility like a manta ray falling from the ceiling, the dark foyer the bottom of the sea and the manta ray watching us from above, halfway between the sea floor and the surface.

Then I heard the Bolognan and the Libyan saying they were fine, and how are you, Mr. Bruno? and Maciste, who wasn't up above anymore and whose voice no longer echoed with infinite shades of fragility, replied:

"Plagued by ailments, my friends, that's the way of it."

And he said this in a voice in which there wasn't a hint of ailing, a voice that boomed in the darkness as if it, the darkness, was a muzzle, and he was straining at it furiously, itching to come out on the porch and gobble up my brother's friends, who just then, the cowards, were saying that their business here was done, they hoped everything would go well, and then they left, wishing us goodnight, Maciste and me, and as they were backing away almost at a run to the garden gate, the door to the house closed and since I didn't see any shadow cross the threshold, I deduced that Maciste had closed the door with some kind of remote control.

Then, for the first time in a long time, I was plunged into total darkness.

What happened next is hard to describe. Maciste's voice guided me to a room on the second floor, lit by a dim bulb half-hidden in a corner. I know I went up some stairs, but I know I went down some stairs too. Maciste's voice was always ahead of me, guiding me. I wasn't afraid. I crossed a dark room with a wall of windows that overlooked the back garden and the tall ivy-covered walls separating the house from the building next door. I felt calm. I opened a door. It wasn't Maciste's room, as I had imagined it would be, but a kind of gym. His private gym, the one my brother's friends had told me about.

I turned on the light. On a wooden table there were several bottles of liniment and various lotions. I took off my jacket and waited. After a while the lights went out. Only then did the door open and I saw Maciste.

X

All of this is hard to describe, as I've said. What happened, what I felt, what I saw. What might have happened, what I might have seen, and what I might have felt. What he felt, I don't know. I'll never know.

He was big and fat. But that wasn't really Maciste. He was big, yes. Tall, broad. He was also fat. He had been a world bodybuilding champion and a tiny part of that glory still lived on somewhere, not in his body, maybe, but in the way he moved. His body was the pallid color of bodies that never see the sun. Either his head was shaved or he had gone totally bald. He was polite. He was wearing an old black robe that fell to his ankles, and sunglasses that looked small on his big face.

I remember that he advanced toward the middle of the gym, where I was standing, his steps so slow that I could tell he was nervous or uncomfortable too.

He asked me how I was, and how old I was. I lied to him, as we had agreed I would, and in turn I asked him why he was called Maciste.

"Are you comfortable?" he asked.

"I'm fine and I'm nineteen. Why do people call you Maciste?"

He felt for a chair and then I knew, without a doubt, that he was blind.

He murmured that in his day he'd played a character called Maciste in a few movies.

I didn't know what to say, not because of his response, but because I realized that I had a blind man in front of me. My brother's friends hadn't warned me about this. Assholes, I thought angrily, and I moved to grab my jacket and go running out of the house. But then I thought: What if they didn't know? Was I going to spoil an ambitious plan, ambitious by our lights, I mean, just because of a mistake? Would my brother be left wandering the streets of Rome just because of a misunderstanding of no consequence in the end, anyway? And what if no one knew that he was blind, or hardly anyone? Because Maciste's life was a mystery, or so I'd been told, and neither the Bolognan nor the Libyan could be said to be part of his inner circle, if such a circle existed.

This was when Maciste said:

"My stage name was Franco Bruno."

And I thought: What?

And he said:

"These days, bodybuilding is considered a sport but when I practiced it, it was an art . . . Like magic . . . There was a time when it was an art and magicians were artists . . . Now it's just a part of the show."

And after a long silence during which I thought about other things, I said:

"I know what you mean." Though in fact I hadn't understood a thing, because as far as I knew Maciste had been an actor and a top bodybuilder, not a magician. Maybe he just felt a kinship with magicians.

And when Maciste heard me he turned his face toward me

and asked if I was naked. I said no, that I had only taken off my jacket.

"Did they explain to you? . . . I need company . . . I don't know whether they explained to you."

I said yes, that they had explained everything. "Don't worry," I said.

Then he took off his robe and I saw him naked for the first time. He said: "Come here and turn out the light."

"The light isn't on," I said.

"Can you see in the dark?"

"More or less," I said.

"Strange—have you always?"

No," I said. "If this had happened to me when I was little, I would have gone crazy. It's only been a little while. Since my parents died in a crash."

"A car crash?"

"Yes. I don't like to talk about it. They died."

"I'm sorry," said Maciste.

We were quiet, each of us sitting in our respective chairs. After a while he asked me whether I wanted something to drink. I said yes.

Maciste left the gym, walking just like anyone. For a few seconds I wondered whether I'd been mistaken, though everybody knows that blind people get around with no trouble in a familiar place.

He came back with a two-liter bottle of Coca-Cola and two mini whiskey bottles, like the kind I knew people got on planes or in hotel minibars. I thought he had forgotten to bring glasses and I waited. When I saw him drink straight from the bottle, I did too.

“Were you driving the car when your parents died?”

It bothered me that he would ask a question like that. I told him that I didn’t know how to drive and that when my parents died I was in Rome, at home, with my brother.

“Interesting,” said Maciste. “And ever since then you can see in the dark?”

“Yes, ever since, or after the second or third day . . .”

“So it’s some kind of psychosomatic thing,” said Maciste.

“I don’t know whether it’s psychosomatic or supernatural, and I don’t care either,” I said.

Then, as I walked over to his chair, a ray of moonlight, fat as a wave, rolled into the gym. Maciste undressed me. He felt my face and my hips and my legs. Then he got up and went to get the bottles of lotion and liniment.

XI

I started to go twice a week to his house on Via Germanico. Sometimes I had to wait a long time outside the door before he let me in. Sometimes we didn't go straight to the gym, and instead he brought me into the kitchen, a kitchen twice as big as our living room, where Maciste made sandwiches for both of us—his specialty—American sandwiches which, according to him, he had been taught to make by an actress named Dolly Plimpton, from Oregon; she had been in the cast of one of his movies, and her recipe consisted of sandwich bread, lettuce, cucumber, tomato, sliced ham, sliced cheese, and various spreads that he could tell apart by the size and shape of the jars and that, mixed, often made the sandwiches taste strange—strong and strange, like the sandwiches you get in airports, he said, but good.

The kitchen was big and it was dirty. Not because it got much use, which it didn't, but because it needed someone to come and give it a deep cleaning, to sweep away the dust that had been gathering in the corners for months, maybe years, but Maciste didn't want to hear it.

The bathroom we used after fucking was the only place in the house that was really clean. The bathtub was huge and instead of a shower curtain it had glass doors, like the kind you see in some movies, doors that Maciste had gotten specially installed, in addition to handrails on the walls that he didn't need, since he moved around the house like someone who could see.

Next to the bathtub there was a little stall with a high-pressure cold-water shower that Maciste called a Norwegian shower. It had a glass door too.

While I showered, Maciste sometimes sat on a wooden stool in the bathroom and ate his sandwiches. We talked about all kinds of things. About my parents' accident and how the loss had affected me (his parents were dead too). About recent movies that I had seen (he'd seen his last movie fifteen years ago). About things that happened next door.

The truth is, I didn't have much to say to him.

When I opened the glass door and saw him eating, it gave me a funny feeling—it was like he was someone else, and I was someone else too, and I didn't like it.

Then I would ask him questions, because the silence he was used to was more than I could stand. So I learned his real name, Giovanni Dellacroce, though *real* only stands for a different kind of unreality, a less random, more fleshed-out unreality, and I learned the exact dates, from before I was born, when he had been crowned Mr. Italy and then Mr. Europe and finally Mr. Universe, which was the first time an Italian had won the world bodybuilding championship, at a competition held in Las Vegas, and I also learned that he'd been to all the great cities of Europe and America (the exact dates: year, month, day), and that he'd been the friend of politicians and famous artists, of movie actresses and soccer players on the national team or for Rome, and that he'd worked on lots of movies, among them the three or four (he was precise about the number, but I've forgotten it) in which he played Maciste, and that sometimes he'd been the good guy and other times, in the end, the bad guy, because that's how it goes, he said, in the beginning you're almost always the good guy and in the end you're always the bad guy.

Other times I tried to go off on my own in the house.

"I'm going to take a walk around your castle," I would say, and hurry off, before he could object or say no.

The house had two floors and it was the biggest house I'd ever seen from the inside (it still is). It was so big that it seemed rooted in the earth. On the second floor there were at least four or five empty rooms. On the first floor was the living room, which Maciste used occasionally, mostly to take naps, and the dining room, which had become a kind of passageway or labyrinth where furniture from other rooms was piled up, cots and mattresses, electric heaters, chairs and tables, wardrobes full of cobwebs, and where there were stacks of old sports or movie magazines. Everything was organized in some way that Maciste never explained to me, though it wasn't hard to figure out that the room's main purpose was to clear obstacles and hazards from other parts of the house.

Then there was the kitchen, which I've already described, and a full bathroom with broken mirrors and a huge gouge in the bathtub. There was also a windowed room that led to the big, crowded foyer, full of useless curtains, and a terrace that led to the back garden and the walls of the neighboring houses. To either side the buildings looked normal, but in back, the houses with entrances on Via degli Scipioni were as silent as Maciste's, no sound of television or radio or children's voices or adults calling to children or to each other. Once I heard the chirp of a cell phone, but only once.

On the second floor, besides the empty rooms, was Maciste's room, big, with its shutters always closed. There was a full-length mirror abandoned in a corner, which Maciste must once have used for daily self-evaluations and possibly also to make love with movie actresses, and a huge bed with a reinforced frame custom-built to support the weight of its owner. Otherwise, the room had a monastic air, of spaciousness and poverty.

Then there were two bathrooms, the big one where I showered and a small one where the last cleaning woman had piled the tools of her trade—a couple of buckets, a mop, several bottles of bleach—before leaving for good, sick of the blind man.

Past the windowed room was the gym where Maciste seemed to spend most of his time, pedaling on a stationary bike or lifting weights, his mind elsewhere, or, more frequently, lying indolently on a long wooden bench in his black robe and sunglasses with a white towel around his neck, thinking about his glory years or maybe—hopefully—thinking about nothing, his mind blank.

Next to the gym was the reading room or library (that's what he called it), in which there wasn't a single book. There were two oil paintings, though. One of them was of Maciste, half-naked, accepting the world bodybuilding championship belt. The other was of Maciste sitting in that very library, behind an oak table that was still there, wearing a suit and tie and with a faint smile on his face, as if he were laughing at the painter and everyone who would ever look at the painting, as if behind everything that surrounded him there was a secret and only he knew it.

Between the two paintings there was a niche holding an icon of St. Pietrino of the Seychelles.

"St. Pietrino of the Seychelles? The Seychelle islands?"

"Yes," said Maciste.

"He went so far away—who is this St. Pietrino?"

"A saint."

"Yes, but what kind of saint? I've never heard of him. It must be a joke."

"No, it isn't a joke," said Maciste. "He's a modern-day Roman saint who was born in Santa Loreto, like me, and one day he went to preach in the Seychelles, that's all."

Since I didn't feel like arguing, I let it go and walked around the house some more. There was no safe anywhere to be seen. I looked for it many times, but I could never find it.

XII

Sometimes, while I was looking for the safe and going from room to room, moving things and putting them back again, I would hear—or rather sense—the presence of Maciste, in his black bathrobe or naked, moving through the darkness of the house following the sound of my footsteps, the almost imperceptible noises I made, until suddenly he would grab me from behind, wrapping me in a bear hug, no matter how careful I tried to be, no matter how stealthy my movements.

And then, when I was in his arms and he was bearing me off through the darkness, or when I was under him or next to him, in the bed or in the gym, every inch of my body slathered with lotion, I would give thanks that I hadn't found the safe, at least not yet.

And sometimes I imagined sleeping there every night, with Maciste, and I imagined hiring a woman to do the cleaning (because in my dreams I didn't intend to be his slave), and convincing him to go out every once in a while, maybe not to the movies but for a walk, like two normal people or two people who pretend to be normal and by pretending actually are normal or become normal, and I saw myself calling a taxi once a week, on Fridays maybe, to come and pick us up and take us to a nice restaurant where we would have a leisurely dinner, with conversation about all kinds of things, or to take us downtown, where I would buy clothes for him at one of those stores for big men, and then clothes for me, and I even imagined myself going to the movies with Maciste, and describing what was on the screen, the way companions of the blind are supposed to.

But the reality is that I hardly ever slept at his house, and also that after dreaming for a while about our life together I would start to wonder where the hell that safe could be.

Late at night, when I got home and my brother and his friends were half-awake, we argued about it. The Bolognan was getting impatient, he said we didn't have all the time in the world, and sometimes he talked about breaking in, armed with a knife or whatever, but when he said this he trembled, he and the Libyan and my brother, the very idea made them tremble, and it wasn't hard for me to steer them back to the original plan.

Other times we talked about Maciste's story, about the movies he'd made that had been such hits. For weeks my brother even looked around the neighborhood video stores and then downtown for the movie called *Maciste vs. the Tartars*, which according to the Bolognan was the best, but he never found it.

I was glad he couldn't find it because I didn't like the idea of seeing Maciste as a young man, when he still had his sight and his hair and a perfect body. I didn't want to see that because I knew what was to come, twenty years later. But once I dreamed about the movie. First, two armies clashed on a dry plain. Then Maciste fought twenty warriors inside a palace and defeated them all. At some point a woman appeared in a tunic of gauzy silk and kissed Maciste. The two of them stood on the edge of a cliff. An abyss yawned at their feet and wisps of smoke rose on the horizon. Then I saw Maciste sleeping in a room with marble walls and a marble floor. And in the dream I thought: this is a movie, he's not really sleeping, he's just pretending to sleep, and in fact he's awake, and only then did I realize that Maciste, making the movie, was in the present, and I, watching the movie or dreaming that I was watching it, was in the future, Maciste's future, or, in other words, nothingness. Then I woke up.

Anyway, I preferred to see him the way he really was when I went to visit him at his house, twice a week.

At the salon things weren't good. Though in some ways they were better than they had been. I was usually exhausted when I got there and sometimes I stumbled through the day like a sleepwalker. Once the boss, who was an understanding woman, pulled me into the bathroom and pushed up my sleeves, looking for needle tracks on my arms.

"I'm not doing drugs," I said.

"What's wrong with you, Bianca? You're looking worse and worse."

"I'm sleeping badly," I said.

It was true. Sometimes I'd go for weeks getting three or four hours of sleep a night.

Once I was tempted to ask Maciste how he lost his sight. The Bolognan and the Libyan had warned me never to raise the subject. According to them, the last person to show any curiosity about Maciste's blindness had ended up with a couple of broken ribs. It wasn't their warning that gave me pause.

I knew Maciste would never lift a hand against me. But there was something that stopped me, something else.

Sometimes I thought it was a good thing that he had gone blind, because that way he would never see me, never see my face, never see the look on my face when I was with him, which wasn't the look of a prostitute or a thief or a spy, but an expectant look, the look of someone hoping for anything and everything, from a kind word to a life-changing declaration.

There weren't many kind words, because Maciste didn't talk much, but there were kind gestures. And there were no life-changing declarations, or at least none I recognized at the time, though since then I've come to remember each of Maciste's words as a key or a dark bridge that surely could have led me elsewhere, as if he were a fortune-telling machine designed exclusively for me, which I know isn't true, though sometimes I like to think so, not often, because I don't lie to myself the way I used to, but every once in a while.

XIII

The rest of the time I spent looking for the safe.

It was a safe that began to seem more and more like an invention of my brother's friends, a safe that existed only in their criminal minds and in their overwrought imaginations—because back then, even if I had a criminal mind too, that didn't mean I let my imagination run wild after something nonexistent.

I wasn't overwrought. In fact, what I felt was a strange stillness, as if before arriving at Maciste's big old house on Via Germanico I had been on the run for months and even years, but from the moment I stepped into his house, from the moment I saw him naked and hulking and white, like a broken refrigerator, everything stopped (or I stopped) and now things were happening at a different speed, an imperceptible speed that was the same as stillness.

Sometimes I looked at them, at my brother and his friends, I looked into their innocent eyes and I was tempted to say:

"The safe exists in only one place—in your fucked-up heads."

But I think I was afraid of convincing them. I was afraid that they would believe me and then there wouldn't be any reason, money aside, for my weekly visit to Maciste's house.

Not that anyone would stop me. And the extra money came in handy. But I knew that to keep visiting him with no ulterior motive would destroy me.

Maciste's eyes—unlike my brother's eyes and his friends' eyes—weren't innocent. He almost always wore sunglasses. But sometimes he would take them off and look at me or pretend to look at me. Then I would shiver and close my eyes and hug him or try to hug him, which was always hard considering his size. One day the Bolognan said to me:

"That bastard is messing with your head. Find the safe and let's get this over with."

He wasn't as dumb as he seemed. And in a way, he was right. The problem was that I couldn't listen to reason anymore. But he was right.

And another time he said:

"Think of the future, think of all the things we have to look forward to in the future."

But there he was wrong. Deep down I was always thinking about the future. I thought about it so much that the present had become part of the future, the strangest part. To visit Maciste was to think about the future. To sweat, to venture into pitch-black rooms, was to think about the future, a future that resembled a room in Maciste's house, but in sharper focus, the furniture covered in old sheets and blankets, as if the owners of the house (a house in the future) had gone away on a trip and didn't want dust to collect on their things. And that was my future and that was how I thought about it, if you can call it thinking (and if you can call it a future).

But most of the time I preferred not to think about anything. I let my mind wander and I spent a long time at one of the windows that overlooked the back garden, naked, my skin still lubricated, watching the night and the stars, the walls of the neighboring houses.

Sometimes I heard a strange sound that split the darkness like a ray of chalk, and Maciste said it was the cry of a hawk that lived in an abandoned house nearby, though I had never heard of a hawk living in a big city, but these things happen in Rome, strange things that were at the time beyond my comprehension and that I easily accepted in a way that today surprises and even repels me: with a shuddering ease, as if leading a life of crime meant always quivering inside, as if leading a life of crime brought with it mingled sensations of immense guilt and pleasure that made me laugh, for example, for no apparent reason at the least appropriate moments, or that plunged me briefly into sadness, a portable sadness that lasted no longer than five minutes and luckily was easy to hide.

At home, meanwhile, everything was the same.

Sometimes, on the nights that I didn't visit Maciste, I left the door open for one of my brother's friends, with the lights off and my eyes closed, since under no circumstances did I want to know which one of them it was, and I made love mechanically, and sometimes I came many times, which caused me to erupt in fierce, unexpected bursts of rage and to cry bitterly.

Then my brother's friend would ask me whether something was wrong, whether I was upset, whether I was hurt, and before he could go on, which would have given away his identity, I would tell him to be quiet or say shhh, and he would stop talking and keep fucking without a word, such was the force of conviction or persuasion or dissuasion that my acts had acquired.

It was an almost supernatural power, I sometimes came to think (though immediately I mocked the idea), making normally talkative people like the Bolognan fall silent, or silent people like the Libyan turn entirely mute, a force that wrested every last question from the mouths of the eternally curious, that created a space of artificial silence and darkness where I could cry and writhe in pain because I didn't like what I was doing, but where I could also come as many times as I wanted and where I could walk (or probe the surface of reality with my fingertips) without false hope, without illusion, not knowing the meaning of it all but knowing the end result, knowing why things are where they are, with a degree of clarity that I haven't had since, though sometimes I sense that it's there, curled up inside of me, shrunken and dismembered—luckily for me—but still there.

XIV

Still, I kept looking for the safe.

I wandered around the house, peering into corners and behind paintings, as my brother and his friends had instructed me, and the safe never turned up.

Only grime, dust, spiders' nests, patches of crumbling wall, patches of old wallpaper protected from the passage of time, lighter, closer to their original color, though upon close examination I was left with the thought that these rectangles were actually more damaged, as if their pallor or their newness was a rare and degenerative disease.

During my forays in search of the safe, the whole house seemed alive. Alive in decay, alive in neglect. But alive.

Let me explain: my own apartment was just an apartment to me. Smaller every day, if anything, with the echoes of thousands of hours of television, sometimes the echo of my father's and mother's voices, but just an apartment. It was dead.

Not Maciste's house. Maciste's house was a promise and a disease, and I spun from promise to disease, feeling on my skin when my body—or the speed impressed on my body—passed from one state to another, the iridescent promise, the disease, an oblique falling or gliding, wandering, touching everything with my fingertips, until I heard Maciste's voice calling me, asking where I was.

Sometimes I didn't answer. I covered my mouth with one hand and breathed through my nose, shallowly, since I knew that, even more silent than me, he would come looking for me, gliding along the dark hallways of the house until he found me by my breathing or the heat of my body, I never knew which, and then everything would start over again.

He grew more generous, and the money that he gave me after each visit gradually increased. Sometimes I followed him, since I imagined he got it directly from the safe, but actually he took it from a drawer in the kitchen, and the amount there was always more or less the same, one hundred and fifty euros, enough to pay me and the woman or teenager (I never saw her, since she came during the day and I came at night) who bought provisions for him at a nearby store and sometimes left him plastic containers of food.

I'm ashamed of this now, but one night I told him that I was in love with him and asked him what his feelings were for me.

He didn't answer. He made me cry out in his gym, but he didn't answer me. Before I left at five that morning, feeling hurt, I told him that things would probably end soon. I told him this in the foyer, with one hand on the doorknob. When I opened the door and let in the light from a streetlamp on Via Germanico, I realized that I was alone.

For days I could only think of him with hatred. To make him angry, during our next meeting, I asked how he had been left blind.

"It was an accident."

"What kind of accident?" I asked.

"A car accident. I was with some friends. Two of them didn't live to tell the story."

"And who was driving?"

Then Maciste focused his blind eyes on my eyes, as if he were really seeing me, and he said that he didn't feel like discussing the subject any further.

I watched him get up with some difficulty and head without hesitation for the open door. I was alone for a long time, lying on the wooden bench, my body smeared with liniment, waiting for him and thinking my own thoughts, about the future that was opening up like a mirror of the present or a mirror of the past, but opening up regardless, until I got bored and fell asleep.

Back then I dreamed a lot and almost all my dreams were quickly forgotten. My life itself was like a dream. Sometimes I stared out a window in Maciste's house and thought about dreams and life, which meant thinking about my own dreams, so quickly forgotten, and my own life, which was like a dream, and I got nowhere, nothing cleared inside my head, but just by doing this, by thinking about dreams and life, a vague weight was lifted from my heart or what I thought of as my heart, the heart of a criminal, of a person without scruples or with scruples so warped that it was hard for me to recognize them as my own.

Then a sigh of relief would escape my throat. I would gasp and smile as if I had just risen from deep waters, out of air, oxygen tanks empty. And immediately I would feel an urge to leave the window and go running in search of a mirror to look at my own face, a face that I knew was smiling and that I also knew I wouldn't like, a fierce and happy face, but my face in the end, my own face, the best among many other distorted faces, a face that emerged from the death of my parents, from my neighborhood where it was always day, and from Maciste's house where I was gambling with my fate, but where my fate for the first time was entirely my own.

None of these certainties—none of these sensations—lasted very long. Thank God, because if they had I would have died or lost my mind.

I was flying high, I was hallucinating, but sometimes my feet were planted firmly on the ground. And then I thought about the safe and the money or the jewels that Maciste had hidden away and the life that awaited us, my brother and me (and also in some way his no-good friends), when we at last got our hands on the treasure, a treasure that was useless to Maciste, since as we saw it all his needs were taken care of and anyway he wasn't young anymore, whereas we had our whole lives ahead of us and we were as poor as rats.

And at moments like these, instead of imagining money, for some reason I imagined gold coins. A safe like Maciste's intestines, black and fathomless, with the gold coins that he had amassed making gladiator movics shining in their depths. It was an exhausting vision. And a pointless one.

One night, as we were making love, Maciste asked me what color his semen was. I was thinking about the gold coins, and for some reason the question seemed pertinent. I told him to pull out. Then I took off the condom and masturbated him for a few seconds. I ended up with a handful of semen.

"It's golden," I said. "Like molten gold."

Maciste laughed.

"I don't think you can see in the dark," he said.

"I can," I said.

"I think my semen is getting blacker by the day," he said.

For a while I pondered what he meant by that.

"Don't worry so much," I told him.

Then I went to shower and when I got back Maciste wasn't in his room. Without turning on the lights, I went looking for him in the gym. He wasn't there either. So I went to the porch room and spent a while there looking out at the garden and the shadow of the neighboring walls.

Maciste's semen wasn't really golden.

I can't remember the exact moment when I realized that I would never see the money, that I would never spend Maciste's treasure on pretty, frivolous things. All I know is that soon after I realized it I closed my eyes and went looking around the rest of the house for Maciste. I found him in the bookless library, sitting under the icon of St. Pietrino of the Seychelles and I climbed astride my lover or my master, it was the same to me, and let him make love to me without saying or feeling a thing.

Before dawn, on my way home in a taxi, I thought I was going to die.

XV

A week without seeing Maciste was like an eternity. But when I tried to imagine an entire life with him I saw nothing: a blank image, the wall of an empty room, amnesia, a lobotomy, my body broken and split into pieces.

At home, meanwhile, things weren't good. My brother seemed dazed, scattered, too thin, and all his friends talked about was the safe.

One morning I said to my brother:

"You're looking more and more messed up."

"Look who's talking," was his answer.

Another day I examined his arms, looking for needle tracks or whatever, just as my boss at the salon had done to me, and all I got was his laugh, a hollow laugh, as if the laughter of our dead parents on that forgotten southern highway was issuing from his throat.

Then I started to be afraid.

"Don't laugh," I said.

"Then don't be ridiculous," he said.

I think we didn't even have the strength to fight anymore.

I asked him another day: "What are you afraid of?"

He didn't answer, but his face said that he was scared of

everything, of his friends, of them living with us, of a future that seemed to hold little, of his sad life as an orphan and a kid without a job.

Another time I heard him crying, locked in the bathroom, as the Bolognan and the Libyan watched TV and made fun of people. Applause, laughter, the Bolognan's sarcastic commentary, and my brother crying quietly in the bathroom, like a humiliated animal seized by cold and fear, which (cold and fear) for him were essentially the same thing. When he came out I asked him discreetly what was wrong. He said nothing, but that night he locked himself in the bathroom again and though this time I didn't hear him crying I sensed that he was on the verge of a breakdown.

But it was hard for me to feel sorry for him, caught as I was between Maciste and the scheming of my brother's friends, who could think of nothing but the safe in the house on Via Germanico. So I can't say I was sorry for him. And that's what I told Maciste, not thinking about what I was saying. I told him that I had found my brother crying and I hadn't felt anything. We had just made love and when I finished saying what I had to say, Maciste turned his huge white face toward me and once again I had the impression that he was looking at me.

"You're going crazy," he said.

I asked him whether he thought that was good or bad. He said it was always bad, except in extreme cases, when going crazy was a way of escaping unbearable pain. And then I told him that maybe I was in unbearable pain, but before he could answer I took it back.

"I'm fine. There's no such thing as unbearable pain. I haven't gone crazy."

One afternoon Maciste got sick and I spent the night taking care of him. He had a fever, but he didn't want the doctor to come. He ordered me to make him a liter of chamomile tea with lemon, which he drank with big spoonfuls of honey, and he went to bed to sweat it out.

When he fell asleep I realized that I would never have another chance like this to look for the safe. So I went in search of it again, room by room. I can't remember when I got the idea that the safe was behind the paintings of Maciste or behind the painting of St. Pietrino of the Seychelles. I took them down one by one, my heart racing. Behind the paintings there was nothing, just the wall in varying stages of deterioration. I also looked in the gym and the bathroom of the gym, checking the tiles (to see if there were any that could be pried up), in the kitchen, under the rugs in the living room and the foyer, behind some useless curtains.

The rest of the night I spent in the living room, sitting in an armchair next to one of the few working lamps in the house, reading magazines and dozing off.

At four in the morning I was woken by the sound of a voice. I went into Maciste's room. He was talking in his sleep. He said something about a street. He said the word *trapeze*. Then he was quiet again. I felt his forehead. He was sweating. That seemed to be a good sign.

For a while I stood there by the door looking at him, deciding whether to go back to the living room. It was then that I knew for sure that I wasn't in love with him. Everything seemed as clear as could be and as entertaining as a TV show and still I was close to tears.

I didn't go back to the living room, but to the gym, where

I smoked and stared into the darkness. Then I got up (I was sitting on the floor of the gym) and walked all around the house, room by room, armed with a flashlight, searching in every corner.

By eight that morning, when the flashlight was no longer necessary, I was sure that there was no safe. Maciste's money, if he had any, was in the bank, not here. That was the end of everything for me.

XVI

Maciste was sick for a week. I took his temperature at night and the fever lingered on endlessly in his massive white body. Once I told him I was going to the pharmacy to buy him aspirin and antibiotics. I asked him to give me the key, because I didn't want him to get up to open the door for me, but he refused, at first tactfully, trying not to hurt my feelings, and then vehemently, as if I didn't know who I was talking to. But I knew very well.

"I just need herbal tea," he said.

I brought him a teapot full of hot water and I left. It was Sunday and there were hardly any people on the train. When I got home, everyone was asleep. I made coffee and then I drank a cup of coffee with milk and I smoked the last cigarette. That night I had a strange dream, though thinking about it now, it wasn't so strange.

I dreamed that Maciste was my boyfriend and we were taking a walk around Campo de' Fiori. At first I was madly in love with him, but as we walked, he didn't seem like such an interesting person to me anymore. He was too fat, too old, too clumsy, the two of us walking arm in arm as kids circled the statue of Giordano Bruno or streamed toward Via dei Giubbonari or

Piazza Farnese, and the crowds in Campo de' Fiori were growing thicker regardless. And then I told Maciste that I couldn't be his girlfriend anymore. And he turned his head toward me and said: all right, all right, so be it, in a whisper that at first seemed to betray a kind of sadness, the faintest hint of despair, but despair nonetheless, which was unusual for him, though later I thought it might have been pride, as if Maciste, deep down, were proud of me.

And then he said goodbye to me. And I was confused, I didn't know what to do, I was afraid to leave him there, in the middle of the Campo de' Fiori crowds, alone and blind, and then I walked away, feeling guilty, but I went, and when I had gone about thirty feet I stopped and watched him, and then Maciste set off, wobbling (because he really was very fat and very big), and was lost among the crowds, though because of his height this took a while to happen, and only after a while did I lose sight of his huge round head.

And that was all. Maciste was gone and I was left alone and I saw myself crying as I crossed Garibaldi Bridge, on my way home. By the time I got to Piazza Sonnino, I was thinking that I had to find a place to go, a place to live, a new job, I had to do things and not die.

And then I woke up and that night I talked to my brother's friends and I told them that Maciste had money but I didn't want to have anything to do with it. I talked about the nonexistent safe. I told them that it did exist. I told them that no one except Maciste could open it, and the only way they could make him open it was by torturing him, and even that was no sure thing, because Maciste could stand worse pain than anything they—pathetic petty criminals—had ever known. Maciste could stand the pain, could live a whole life sunk in pain.

My brother's friends listened to me in silence, shaken by the path I was revealing to them. Or by the terrible path they could see for themselves.

And then the sun began to come up and I had breakfast, took a shower, and went out. I went walking to Via Germanico. Maciste wasn't in bed yet. If he was surprised to see me at that time of day, I don't know. I told him I had come to visit him for the last time. In fact, I hadn't come to visit, because that in some sense presumed nudity, sex, long hours of silence in the dark house, but to say goodbye, because I didn't plan to come back ever again.

"Are you going on a trip?"

"Yes," I said. "I'm going to start a new life."

He didn't ask me where I planned to go. He told me to wait for a minute. When he came back he gave me an envelope full of money.

"Thank you," I said as I left the envelope on a shelf, trying not to make the slightest noise. I knew that Maciste wouldn't be surprised when he found it there.

Then I went to the salon and, after talking to the boss, I took the day off and wandered around the city. At dusk I went home. The Bolognan and the Libyan were watching TV, but anyone observing them carefully would have realized that they were far away. Not in our living room, but in a bus station or at an airport. Not under our light, but bathed in a red glow that seemed to emanate from another planet.

My brother was watching TV too, sitting in a chair, behind the couch. I made coffee for the four of us and served it to them, then I told them that they had to leave. They acted as if they hadn't heard. But my brother didn't argue either and then I knew I had won.

After a while I told them again to leave. They could watch the end of the show and then they had to pack their suitcases and get out.

"Where are we supposed to go?" asked the Bolognan.

I stared at him as if my face was raw flesh and his was raw flesh too.

"To Maciste's house," I answered. "Everything is over. As soon as the show ends I want you to go."

And when the show had ended—I watched it all the way through, not even missing the commercial breaks—I planted myself in the middle of the living room and turned off the TV and they looked at me without getting up from the couch and I said that I was going out for a walk around the neighborhood and that I might pass by the police station, and when I came back I didn't want to see them here.

And then I told my brother to come with me and surprisingly my brother got up and came. We walked around Trastevere until late into the night.

"Are we going to the police?" asked my brother.

I said that I didn't think it would be necessary. We went into a bar and ordered sandwiches and coffee. We talked about any old thing.

When we got back home his friends were gone.

"I hope I never see them again in my life," said my brother, then he shut himself in his room and cried.

That night, for the first time in a long time, night was really night, dark and fragile and edged with fears, and it was the weak and the weary who sat up awake, eager to see the dawn again, the shimmering light of Piazza Sonnino.

For days, though, I was on the alert for bad news. I read the paper (not every day, because we didn't have enough money to buy the paper every day), I watched TV, I listened to the news on the radio at the salon, afraid of coming across a final shot of Maciste sprawled on the ground, in a pool of blood (his cold blood), and alongside it ID photos of the Bolognan and the Libyan, staring at me nostalgically from the page or from the screen of our TV set (which was really ours now, not our dead parents'), as if these pictures—of killers and victim, killer and victims—were evidence that outside the storm still raged, a storm not located in the skies of Rome, but in the European night or the space between planets, a noiseless, eyeless storm from another world, a world that not even the satellites in orbit around the Earth could capture, a world where there was a place that was my place, a shadow that was my shadow.